D1551036

MISSIONS OF THE U.S.
AIR FORCE
COMBAT CONTROLLERS

BY MARCIA AMIDON LUSTED

Published by The Child's World®
1980 Lookout Drive • Mankato, MN 56003-1705
800-599-READ • www.childsworld.com

Acknowledgments
The Child's World®: Mary Berendes, Publishing Director
Red Line Editorial: Design, editorial direction, and production
Photographs ©: Tech. Sgt. Michael R. Holzworth/U.S. Air Force, cover, 1;
Tech Sgt. John Hughel/U.S. Air Force, 5; Staff Sgt. Tony R. Ritter/U.S. Air
Force, 6; Tech Sgt. Phil Speck/U.S. Air National Guard, 8; U.S. Army, 10; Staff
Sgt. Jeremy T. Lock/U.S. Air Force, 12; Eric J. Tilford/U.S. Navy, 14; Tech.
Sgt. Jacob N. Bailey/U.S. Air Force, 16; Staff Sgt. Desiree N. Palacios/U.S. Air
Force, 18; Master Sgt. Jeremy Lock/U.S. Air Force, 20

ISBN 9781634074421

LCCN 2015946360

Printed in the United States of America
Mankato, MN
December, 2015
PA02285

TABLE OF
CONTENTS

ABOUT THE U.S. AIR FORCE COMBAT CONTROLLERS

- **Combat** Controllers started out as Army Pathfinders during World War II (1939–1945). They were needed to help find good places to bring troops more supplies. They also helped report on weather at landing sites.

- When the Air Force became its own part of the military, the Pathfinders became the Combat Controllers in 1953. Today they are a vital part of any special military mission.

- The motto of the United States Air Force Combat Controllers is "First There." And they usually are the first ones on the scene.

- Combat Controllers are part of special operations forces.

areas. And they learn how to search areas to see how dangerous they are.

Once training is over, controllers can go on missions with any branch of the U.S. military. The men stand tall and proud. Their work is about to begin. These Combat Controllers will enter combat situations. They will fight **terrorists**. They will save lives during natural disasters. Combat Controllers are some of the best operators on the planet. And now their skills are ready to be tested.

◀ Combat Controllers are taught how to scout, or check out, an area to make sure it is safe.

Chapter 2

BATTLE OF KHAM DUC

Kham Duc was an important **airstrip** in South Vietnam. Americans fought a battle here in 1968 during the Vietnam War (1954–1975). They fought against North Vietnamese and other forces that wanted to gain control of the area.

The Combat Controllers were the first ones into the area. They planned to help clear destroyed planes and equipment that were blocking the airstrip. Then

U.S. forces could use it. But as they flew into the area, they were under heavy enemy fire. Some U.S. troops left the area. Others moved to bases where they were needed for other missions. There were only two days left to get 1,500 people out. In two days the North Vietnamese Army would arrive. There would be heavy fighting.

The controllers guided huge **cargo** planes and helicopters to land and pick up troops. The controllers even directed U.S. airplanes to bomb the enemy. They did all of this while under enemy fire. Enemy bombs exploded U.S. Jeeps and other equipment. Injured people had to be moved under cover and then onto waiting planes. Smoke billowed into the sky as one plane sat burning on the **runway**.

North Vietnamese forces were closing in. Three Combat Controllers crouched beside the runway. They were the last people left. Finally a plane landed to take them out. The enemy kept firing. The plane thumped, bumped, and then took off into the sky. The controllers were safe.

Chapter 3

RESCUE IN AFGHANISTAN

It was April 11, 2005. A group of Combat Controllers was assigned to Afghanistan. Their mission was to rescue an Afghan general who worked with the United States. He and his men had been attacked by enemy forces. A quick response team was given the mission.

Helicopters carried the team to a place near the attack. Gunships provided protection when the team landed. Enemy bullets panged off the metal of the aircraft. But the team landed safely. The soldiers searched through half-ruined buildings. Finally the Afghan general was found. The controllers helped him outside. The enemy began firing at them from hidden areas.

Enemy fire injured one controller's foot. His comrade was injured badly in both legs. They were trapped in an area apart from the rest of their team. The soldier got on his radio. He provided air traffic control for all U.S. aircraft in the area. At the same time, he fired at enemy soldiers. And he kept helping his wounded friend.

One of the U.S. helicopter pilots radioed back. The man on the other end had bad news. Enemy soldiers were coming up a nearby hill. The soldier knew he needed to get himself and his comrade out. He helped guide the helicopter pilot. It landed between the U.S. team and the enemy. The fighting went on for four hours. Then the wounded soldier and several others made it into the helicopter. As they pulled away into the sky, bullets bounced and thudded against the sides of the craft. Later they would find 55 bullet holes in that helicopter. But they made it out.

Chapter 4

FIGHTING AL-QAEDA

A raging battle was taking place in Herat Province, Afghanistan. Bullets and grenades swirled through the air. They raised puffs of dust as they hit the ground. It was October 5, 2009. Special Forces troops had moved in. Combat Controllers were part of the group. Their mission was to capture the second most important al-Qaeda leader in the area.

Al-Qaeda was responsible for the September 11, 2001, attacks on the United States. On that day, terrorists crashed two airplanes into the towers of the World Trade Center in New York City. Another plane crashed into the Pentagon in Washington, DC. A fourth plane crashed in Pennsylvania. These crashes killed many Americans.

The U.S. troops entered a village in Herat Province. They had avoided roads planted with mines. They stormed a building where the leader was supposed to be. But suddenly they were facing heavy enemy gunfire.

But help was on the way. The Combat Control team had set up a base to help U.S. aircraft enter the area without being shot down. They told the aircraft to stay a certain distance away. Otherwise the noise of the engines would warn al-Qaeda that U.S. troops were coming. Under enemy fire, Combat Controller Staff Sgt. Robert Gutierrez, Jr. was also managing many combat planes at once. He directed them where to fire. He told them to drop **flares** to confuse al-Qaeda fighters. But suddenly a bullet hit him in the chest near his lungs. It was hard for him to breathe. He was badly injured.

15

Gutierrez kept controlling aircraft while a medic worked on him. He lost half the blood in his body. Meanwhile U.S. aircraft sprayed bullets across the area and killed the al-Qaeda commander. Then Gutierrez directed them to help get the Special Forces men out. He guided the rescue helicopters to the right location. He kept giving reports to all the pilots until he passed out. Gutierrez was taken to safety to recover.

Gutierrez was awarded the Air Force Cross for his actions. It is the second highest military award in the United States. Even with his severe injuries, he and Combat Controllers helped save the lives of all the men with him. Not a single U.S. soldier was killed during the attack.

◄ Combat Controller Staff Sgt. Robert Gutierrez, Jr. shakes hands with Defense Secretary Leon E. Panetta after being awarded for his actions.

Chapter 5

RESCUING HAITI

It was January 2010. A terrible earthquake struck Haiti, a country that shares an island with the Dominican Republic. Many people were killed. Buildings were destroyed. Haiti needed help. But the control tower for its airport had also been destroyed in the earthquake. How could rescue and relief planes land on the island without it?

The first 72 hours after an earthquake are important. People can still be rescued from fallen buildings. But rescuers had no way to get to Haiti. Planes that did reach the airport without help from the control tower were landing everywhere. There was a lot of confusion. Runways were clogged. There were only two fuel trucks to fuel the planes. The Combat Controllers would be the first rescue workers to get to Haiti. They would reopen the airport. They arrived the day after the earthquake.

Lt. Colonel Brett Nelson said that his men walked off the airplane with little more than the radios on their backs. Just minutes later they were talking to incoming airplanes. Then the controllers searched through the rubble. They looked for survivors. They dug beneath piles of concrete and furniture. The Combat Controllers found seven people who were still alive. They brought them carefully to safety and gave them medical care. Combat Controllers made sure that the runways and other airport equipment were safe. They set up landing lights on the runway. Because they could not use the control tower, they set up a table next to the runway. They guided planes in and out from there. By the end of the first day, 44 airplanes had landed.

19

- Their mission is to get to combat zones first and without being seen.

- They establish airfields or assault zones, and they control air traffic. They also fight, perform rescues, and collect intelligence information.

Chapter 1

THE BEST OPERATORS ON THE PLANET

An Air Force plane thunders across the sky. Airmen toss motorcycles out of the plane's rear door. Each motorcycle has a parachute. The parachutes open against the blue sky. A green light in the plane flashes. "Go!" Immediately, U.S. Air Force Combat Controllers also parachute from the plane. When they reach the ground, they find the motorcycles. The bikes rev to life. The men quickly race to where they need to set up an airfield. It will be a place for planes to land. It will be in a combat zone. Battles will be taking place there.

Air Force Combat Controllers aren't often in the news. But these controllers are the best at what they do. They know how to set up airfields. They tell air and ground traffic where to go. This way, bombs don't hit friendly people or troops. They also know how to carry out secret missions, fight enemies, and perform rescues.

Being part of the Combat Controllers Team (CCT) takes months of training. Not just anyone can be in this group. Only men can apply. They must be young and in shape. They must pass a background check. It is important that they can be trusted with secret information. Then training begins.

Recruits have to pass tough swimming, running, and exercise tests. They are pushed to their limits so they can handle anything that comes their way. They also have to learn about aircraft, air traffic control, weapons, weather, and communications. They jump out of planes. They learn how to scuba dive into combat

In the days to follow, the skies were crowded with airplanes circling and waiting to land. The smell of jet exhaust covered the area. The rumble of engines was deafening. In one day they landed 600 planes. The Combat Controllers had to start limiting the numbers of planes that could land. Usually the airport in Haiti handled only three planes a day. They had to decide which planes were the most important. They would let those land first. There were so few fuel trucks that it was difficult to refuel airplanes. There were also only two tow vehicles to move planes and cargo around the airport. One huge plane got stuck on the runway, waiting for fuel. It blocked traffic for hours.

Despite these challenges, the Combat Controllers were key in getting Haiti's airport back into operation. Soon planes were landing smoothly and quickly. Because the Combat Controllers were able to set everything up, planes were able to bring food, water, medical supplies, and relief workers. They went right to work helping the people of Haiti.

◄ A combat controller uses a rangefinder to find a place for planes to land outside of Port-au-Prince, Haiti.

GLOSSARY

airstrip (airstrip): An airstrip is a strip of ground that is meant for airplanes to take off and land on. Combat Controllers helped lead planes to the airstrip.

cargo (KAHR-goh): Cargo is any goods or equipment that are carried on a ship, airplane, or truck. Combat Controllers guided cargo planes.

combat (KAHM-bat): Combat is fighting between people or armies. Combat Controllers' mission is to get to combat zones first and without being seen.

flares (flairz): Flares are devices that make a bright fire or light and are used as signals. Combat Controller Staff Sgt. Robert Gutierrez, Jr. directed other controllers where to drop flares.

recruits (ri-KROOTs): Recruits are people who have recently joined the armed forces. The recruits trained to become U.S. Air Force Combat Controllers.

runway (RUHN-way): A runway is a strip of level ground that aircraft can land on and take off from. The runway was clogged until the Combat Controllers helped planes land.

terrorists (TER-ur-ists): Terrorists are people who use violence and threats to gain power or force a government to do something. Al-Qaeda terrorists attacked New York City on September 11, 2001.

TO LEARN MORE

Books

Goldish, Meish. *Air Force: Civilian to Airman.* New York: Bearport Publishing, 2011.

Loria, Laura. *Air Force.* New York: Gareth Stevens Publishing, 2011.

Stilwell, Alexander. *Air Force Combat Controllers: What It Takes to Join the Elite.* New York: Cavendish Square Publishing, 2014.

Web Sites

Visit our Web site for links about missions of the U.S. Air Force Combat Controllers: childsworld.com/links

Note to Parents, Teachers, and Librarians: We routinely verify our Web links to make sure they are safe and active sites. So encourage your readers to check them out!

SELECTED BIBLIOGRAPHY

"Air Force Combat Controllers 'Rockin' on the Mike,' Making Things Happen." *Talking Proud.* Talking Proud Archives, 6 August 2006. Web. 4 June 2015.

"Combat Controllers." *U.S. Air Force.* Official United States Air Force Website, 18 August 2010. Web. 7 June 2015.

Patterson, Thom. "Combat Air Controllers: Skydiving with Dirt Bikes and Guns." *CNN.* Cable News Network, 22 June 2014. Web. 5 June 2015.

INDEX

ABOUT THE AUTHOR

Marcia Amidon Lusted is the author of more than 100 books and 500 magazine articles for young readers. She is also a writing instructor and an editor.